From Tom.

To. Margate

183, Great Junction St,
Leith
Edin 6.

Nell was dragged through the water (page 20)

HOW NELL SCORED

BY

BESSIE MARCHANT

THOMAS NELSON AND SONS, LTD.
LONDON, EDINBURGH, NEW YORK
TORONTO, AND PARIS

THOMAS NELSON AND SONS LTD
Parkside Works Edinburgh 9
3 Henrietta Street London WC2
312 Flinders Street Melbourne C1
5 Parker's Buildings Burg Street Cape Town

THOMAS NELSON AND SONS (CANADA) LTD
91–93 Wellington Street West   Toronto 1

THOMAS NELSON AND SONS
19 East 47th Street New York 17

SOCIÉTÉ FRANÇAISE D'EDITIONS NELSON
25 rue Henri Barbusse Paris V^e

CONTENTS

HOW NELL SCORED

CHAPTER I

"THE BANDALINA STAR"

" Now, Sue, be a sport, and give them a good send-off. Mother is not to see any tears before she goes, remember that. You can howl yourself black in the face afterwards if it so pleases you." Nell Draycot swung her sister round by the shoulders as she spoke, and gave her a vigorous shake by way of emphasis.

" I truly won't cry, Nell, only I could not help feeling a bit gulpy," answered Sue with a strangled sob. " It will seem so utterly horrid to have father and mother away together; it would not be so bad if David were at home."

Sue's shoulders heaved with a sort of convulsive gasp, which brought her another shaking from Nell.

Just then came a shout from the house, and the two girls who had been harnessing the pair of horses to the best wagon, a light, four-wheeled affair, which had been recently painted, hurried to lead the spirited animals to the door of the little wooden house, where their mother was waiting ready for the start, and their father was busy bringing out the baggage, which he stowed in the back of the wagon.

" Sue, you had better ride with us as far as the lower gate, then I shan't have to get down," said Mr. Draycot, as he climbed up to the driver's seat and took the rope reins from Nell, who was keeping the frisky pair as quiet as she could, so that her mother should not be frightened by their prancing.

" I will go with you, then Sue can help Aunt Angelina Ann get on with the churning." Nell spoke with crisp decision, then climbing up beside her father, she hung on somehow, while those very lively horses tore across the home paddock as if they were running a race. She was dreadfully behind with the morning's work, and going to the lower gate would hinder her a full half-hour, but she had seen that Sue was having hard work to keep the tears back, and she did not mean that her mother should be saddened at the start if she could avoid it.

It was quite late last evening when a message had come by telephone, that David was lying ill at New Plymouth, and his father and mother were asked to come to him at once.

Mr. and Mrs. Draycot would have started that night, but the track over the lower spurs of Mount Egmont was too bad for even New Zealand horses to follow at night. So the anxious parents had to wait for dawn. David was the eldest son, then came Nell, and Sue, while Ned, an urchin of twelve years old, completed the family.

Nell chattered cheerfully all the way to the lower gate. She gave her mother all sorts of messages for David, urging him to buck up and get well as soon as possible.

She was talking for the sake of saying something,

and she was thankful when the lower gate was reached
and she could slip from the wagon, wave a cheery
good-bye to the travellers, and then be free for a
minute of breakdown, if she felt like it.

The trouble was that when she began to howl she
never knew when to leave off, so, all things considered,
it seemed wiser not to begin. She marched back to
the house with her head well up and whistling blithely.
Mentally she had turned her back on David and the
troubles, and was concentrating on the day's work. It
would take her father and mother two days of driving
to reach New Plymouth. Even if David was better,
they would need to stay two days to rest the horses,
so at the least it would be six days before they could
get home again.

Ned was at school at Blackwell, six miles away—he
went on Monday mornings and came back Friday
evenings; it was Wednesday now, so it would not be
long to wait. Meanwhile she and Sue and Aunt Angelina Ann, who was their father's aunt, had the place
to themselves. But there was the telephone linking
them up with the post office at Lupton, and that was a
huge comfort.

Of course Sue was crying when Nell got back, and
the sound of the dreary sobbing made Nell feel as if
she would like to slap her sister for being so silly.
Instead, she hurried off to go the round of the sheep in
the farther paddock. She caught one animal that had
been attacked with fly, and deftly throwing the kicking,
struggling creature, she dressed the affected part and
let it go again. The two dogs were with her, and they
did their work in the quick and clever manner which
was a sort of second nature with them.

me to go a bit farther when necessary. Anyhow, I should not rest in my bed with you wandering alone on the shore at night in this sort of weather. My word, how it blows! I'm ready; come along, old thing."

Clinging together they made their way across the little paddock, and out on to the cliff, whence a steep path went down to the shore.

" Don't go down, you will see as much from here," urged Sue; and because she knew this was true, Nell stood still, sending her gaze searching over the dark heaving waters for a sight of the craft they had seen earlier in the evening.

" Nothing doing; at least I can't see a sign of her," she said presently, heaving a sigh of relief. " Can you see anything ? "

" No, I can't, and I did not expect to," said Sue in a rather petulant tone. " Come along, Nell, it is weird out here at night. I wish we had brought the dogs. Yah, I am downright afraid."

" What are you afraid of—your own shadow ? " scoffed Nell in laughing tones. " I am thinking you will not even see that with such heavy clouds overhead; it is really very dark on land, although it seems lighter on the water. How the wind blows ! "

" And how it rains ! " cried Sue, clinging tightly to her sister. " Come along, old thing, or we shall be wet through."

They were very damp by the time they had struggled across the paddock, but they pulled off their clothes and tumbled into bed as quickly as they could. Sue was asleep almost as soon as her head touched the pillow, but Nell kept starting up, thinking that she heard something. Even when she did drop into slumber her dreams were frightful: she was battling with wind and rain, she was in the sea battling with great waves, and finally she fell headlong down a tremendous precipice, and awoke suddenly to find herself sitting on the floor, with the new day looking in at the window.

" Oh, I am glad it is morning ! " she exclaimed with a shiver; then rousing Sue, she made a hasty and rather a sketchy toilet, and whistling for the dogs started to go round the sheep before breakfast.

She did not get very far. There were a hundred and forty ewes in the west paddock. She had just succeeded in making the number right after one or two false starts, and she was going on over the hill to the long strip of waste land all encumbered with ti-tree scrub, which was the nearest way to the big paddock, when an uproar of barking from the younger of the two dogs sent her off in a hurry shorewards to see what was the matter.

She cried out in horror and dismay when she reached the top of the cliff, for a vessel, a complete and total wreck, was piled on the rocks down below, and plain to be seen was the name of her in black letters on a white ground—*The Bandalina Star*.

CHAPTER II

SAVED FROM THE WRECK

NELL's first impulse was to run away. The sight of that tangled mass of spars and sails piled on the rocks, with the ship lying on its side, frightened all the strength and courage out of her. Then she remembered that her father was away, and that she herself was the man of the family for the time. If there was any living thing out there on those black bristling rocks, then it was up to her to find it and rescue it if she could.

It was low tide now ; in a couple of hours or so the wreck would be under water again, so what had to be done must be done quickly. It was no use even to go back to the house to fetch Sue, who was two years younger, and no more courageous than she was herself. It would take a full twenty minutes to get to the homestead, even if she ran all the way, and then there would be twenty minutes to come back, and all that time the tide would be flowing in. Plainly what had to be done she must do, and that quickly. Calling to the dogs to come to her help, for they would be useful in searching, she plunged down the steep bit to the shore, slipping, sliding, and finishing up with a scrambling roll which brought her down to the strip of stony beach nearly, but not quite, head first.

The dogs rushed on ahead, barking wildly, as if they understood that there was disaster, and were anxious to do their part to put things right again.

Presently, as if in answer to the noisy barking of the dogs, Nell heard a shout for help, and yelling back at the top of her voice, she broke into a run as she struggled down the shingly beach to the great mass of rocks which, covered at high tide, were such a menace to shipping venturing near the land.

She ran round to the other side of the wreck, but could see nothing. "Where are you?" she shouted, wondering how she would manage to get a foothold on those slippery rocks if she had to climb up on to the boat, which was a coasting smack.

"I am up here jammed in the wreckage," answered a voice so shrill with suffering that it sounded almost like a woman's voice. "There is another man here too, but he is pretty far gone."

"Two of them!" said Nell to herself as she began to scramble upwards. "I can't get two men down alone before the tide comes in. I must send the dogs to fetch Sue here. Help! go bring your master quick —quick, bring your master!"

Help, a shaggy young dog, cocked his head on one side, gave a yelp of understanding, and turning shorewards, started off in the direction of the house; but the old dog stood at the foot of the slippery rocks uttering little whimpering noises, as if fully aware of the trouble, and anxious to help.

Nell, scrambling over the rocks, had reached the side of the boat, and, clambering upwards by means of the tangled wreckage, managed to reach the steep slope of the deck, where, almost hidden by the welter of spars and stays, a man lay pinned down, and unable to help himself.

" Why, it is a girl ! " he exclaimed in a tone of deep disgust, as Nell, in her old blue jersey and short serge skirt, came into view.

" A girl is better than nothing when one is in a fix like yours," she remarked in a cheery, matter-of-fact tone as she scrambled over the tangle of rubbish to reach him. " Can you tell me where I can find a saw or a chopper to clear some of this muddle away and get you free ? "

" There is a saw in the cabin, and there is a meat-chopper in the galley," he answered, his voice trailing off in a groan. Then he roused himself to say with an effort : " There is another man aboard, and his is a worse plight than mine, I'm afraid. Look after him first."

" Oh, one at a time is my motto ; when I have got you free, there will be two of us to do things," called back Nell as she crawled across the deck to reach the galley. It took her a few minutes to find the chopper ; then she crawled back to the man, who kept groaning from impatience at his helplessness, and also from the pain of his hurts.

She started to hack away at the rubbish, but it took time, and she had only just succeeded in getting him clear when a short bark from the old dog, and a noisy yelping in the distance, announced the coming of Help with Sue.

" It is no use, I can't stand ; my leg is broken," said the man in despairing tones as she dragged him clear and propped him up so that he did not roll down the steep slope of the deck.

" If you can't walk you will have to ride," she answered rather breathlessly, for it had been stiff work to chop him clear ; then she scrambled up the steep slope of the deck so that she could look over and see her sister, who was coming down the beach with Help careering wildly in front, and she sent out her voice in a lusty shout, " Sue, Sue, don't come any farther ; run home as fast as you can go, harness the old horse to the little cart as quickly as you can, and bring them down here. There is a man on board who can't walk, and we have got to get him out of this before the tide covers the rocks. Hurry up ! "

Sue was away like a streak, no need to tell her to hurry ; only too well she understood the danger of delay. There was a man who could not walk to save himself ; that meant that Nell would not leave him, so Nell would be in danger too. Fear lent wings to Sue's feet ; she must get that old horse harnessed, and she must bring horse and cart down to the rocks in the quickest possible time.

" Where is the other man ? " asked Nell sharply as she scrambled back to the lower side of the deck.

" Over yonder ; he had gone to get himself a life-belt when we heaved on to these rocks," said the man, and Nell started on a creeping progress which was some-thing after the nature of walking up the roof of a house.

She found the man, whose face was white and pinched, while there was a blue tinge round his mouth that gave him a very ghastly appearance ; but he was not dead, for he cried out for help as she came near.

He was so held down that he could not move his head, but his legs were free, and Nell heaved a little sigh of satisfaction ; at least he would be able to walk, and perhaps he would be able to help lift the man whose leg was hurt. Again she had to chop with all her might to get him clear, but she managed to free him. He was on his feet and groping his way through the tangle so that he could get ashore, when she pulled him up sharply, telling him that he would have to help her lift the other man over the side, and lower him on to the rocks, so that they could get him to safety before the tide ran in.

He came reluctantly to her assistance. He was not a very big man, but he was built for strength, and Nell marvelled at the ease with which he lifted the poor fellow whose leg was hurt ; but all the time he looked ghastly ill, and every time he lifted he let out a louder groan than the man who was hurt.

Sue was coming with the horse and cart. But the tide was coming in so fast that it was already washing round the ankles of Nell as she leaped down from the slippery rocks, and stood ready to receive the hurt man, whose name was Jim Peters, as the other man lowered him from the wreck. Jim, who had a rope round his body under his arms, helped himself a great deal by gripping on to ropes or any bit of the wreck to which he could cling, so that he was not a dead weight on the man above. But the torture he endured must have been awful, and when at last Nell caught him in her arms as he was lowered down to her, he just swooned and lay as if he was dead.

" Oh, make haste, make haste," she called urgently to the man still on the wreck. " The water is all round us, and you must help hold him up until Sue gets here."

There was no answer from the man on board, and Nell crouched on the shingle, holding up the head of the man who had fainted, while the dogs barked wildly, and Sue shouted to the horse to make it go faster.

" We shall never reach the shore if we are not quick," she cried.

" I'm so sorry I was so long," said Sue, who was still short of breath from the haste she had made. " Oh, Nell, is the poor man dead ? "

" No, he has fainted," said Nell shortly. " Now the other one will be drowned if he does not come quickly, for I am not going to climb up there again. But however we are going to get this man into the cart alone I cannot imagine, he is so dreadfully heavy."

" I will back Bowler round here ; then we can hoist him on the rock and slide him on to the cart."

Sue was splashing round with great vigour as she talked, and had just got the cart backed close to where Nell was supporting Jim, when the other man appeared, let himself down from the wreck with the agility of a monkey, and was ready to help lift Jim Peters into the cart.

" Why did you not come straight down when I called you ? " asked Nell in a severe tone.

" I slipped into the cabin to see if I could find where the captain kept his money, and I have got it too," said the man, slapping his side with great satisfaction, and then Nell noticed that he had a bag slung round him under his arm.

" Oh, are you that sort ? " she said with a scornful intonation, and then she took no more notice of him, busying herself with getting Jim settled as comfortably as she could.

" The captain was washed overboard," volunteered
the man, as if in defence of his action.

" You will have to push, and push hard," jerked out
Nell. " Go to the other wheel, and push at the spokes
to help the horse ; it is frightful work getting the cart
through this shingle, and we have to make haste.
Sue, get the old horse along as fast as you can ; we
shall have a struggle for it."

She was right ; they did have a struggle. Both dogs
were swimming. Sue was up to her waist in water,
clinging to the horse, shouting encouragement to the
poor beast ; but Nell did not utter a sound except to
cry out sharply to the man at the other wheel, telling
him to put more force into his push.

" We shall never get the cart through ; I shall swim
for it," sobbed the man, who seemed to be beside
himself with sheer funk.

" If you let go your hold of the cart, you will be
swept away by the eddy and drowned," said Nell, who
was breathless from her hard work at the wheel.   Then
she added contemptuously, " And it will serve you right,
too, for thinking more of your own safety than of the
safety of the poor man who cannot help himself."

" You got it smack in the face that time, Serge
Dobbin, and it jolly well served you right," said the
man in the cart, with a hoarse chuckle that ended in a
groan as the wheels of the cart bumped over some rocks
with horrible shaking of the springless vehicle.

Serge made no more attempt at saving himself alone.
Instead, he put out his strength to such an extent that
he fairly forced the cart through the shingle, and the
horse broke into a shambling trot as the weight of the
cart came pushing against it.

" Hurrah, hurrah, we shall do it ! " cried Sue, with a waggly sort of cheer as they scrambled over the rough shingle, hitting the rocks they had no time to avoid. The dogs broke into wild barking and shot ahead, reaching the shore in front of the others.

Coming in the straight line from the rocks, however, they had to cross a dip in the ground where great rocks were half-buried by shingle. The water was deeper here ; Sue was in almost to her waist, and the wheels of the cart sank so deeply that it required every atom of strength that Nell and the man called Serge could put forth to get the wheels round. But it was only for a few yards, and then they would have reached dry land.

Nell was straining every muscle ; she was just putting every bit of strength into her push to carry them over the bad part when suddenly her foot slipped, and at that moment a big wave, curling in, caught her and tore her from her hold of the wheel. She was caught by the eddy, only realizing her own danger by the shriek of anguish that came from Sue.

CHAPTER III

AUNT ANGELINA ANN TAKES HOLD

NELL flung out her arm as she was torn from her hold of the wheel, and it was caught in a grip as of steel and held ; she was dragged through the water as the cart lurched and bumped, her groping feet found firm ground under her, the water drained from her face so that she could open her eyes, there was a fresh lurch of the cart as if it had been most violently pushed from behind, the old horse scrabbled with its feet in the shingle, and they were above the reach of the water.

Then Nell cried out in amazement to see that it was Jim Peters, the man with the broken leg, who had saved her by reaching out and gripping her as she was caught by the wave.

" Are you hurt ? " he asked. His face was grey and drawn from the torture of his sudden movement, but his voice was full of concern for her, and he seemed to have forgotten his own pain.

" I don't think so," she answered, managing to smile at him. " The breath was nearly knocked out of me, and when I heard Sue scream I realized that the eddy had got me. If you had not held me so fast I should have been carried away too quickly for any chance to save myself—sucked down by the undertow."

" Glad I was able to do something," growled Jim. " It has been a bit thick, I can tell you, to have to be saved from the wreck by a couple of kids like you and your sister. Oh, you need not mind being called kids ; though you do look so grown up you've only got kid strength, though you have woman sense and more than woman courage. Hallo ! what has happened to Serge ? "

He might well ask, for at this moment Serge seemed to crumple like a house of cards, and he dropped to the ground looking so much like a dead man that Nell cried out in dismay as she hurried to the place where he had fallen.

Over him she stooped with very lively fear in her heart ; but he was breathing right enough, although in a noisy, stertorous fashion.

" What is it, Nell ? " cried Sue, coming to bend over him too. " Is he in a fit, do you think ? "

" What I think is that he has just tuckered out," replied Nell. " I expect he overdid himself in pushing the cart, but it is certain that we should never have got through from the rocks if he had not, for the tide is running in so fast. Do you think we can heave him into the cart, Sue, and get him home ? He will die if he is left lying out here."

" I thought it was bad for people to move them when they are unconscious like this," said Sue nervously. Of choice she would rather not have had to touch the man with his awful white face that was blue-shadowed round eyes and mouth.

" It would certainly be bad for him to leave him lying where he is, for the tide is not nearly in yet," answered Nell ; then she turned to Jim and said,

" Do you think it would hurt you very much if we put him in beside you ? "

" I guess I can put up with it if you will move my leg a bit for me," he answered. " I can even help you lift him in, if you will get him so that I can get a grip on his collar. I'm pretty strong in the arm."

" Indeed you are, or I should not have been here now," Nell said with a quick and grateful glance at him ; then she and Sue managed to hoist Serge up so that Jim could get one hand fixed in his collar, after which the lifting was fairly easy, and the limp form of Serge was propped up beside Jim in the cart.

The rest of the journey to the house was straight enough, and they found Aunt Angelina Ann standing at the door waiting for them, while kettles were boiling and beds ready for the rescued.

The unloading was a simple process, carried out under instruction from Jim. A wheelbarrow was brought, Serge was dragged into it, and the united strength of the household got the barrow into the house and into the bedroom ; Serge was dragged from the barrow to the bed, and they left him lying there while they went out to repeat the process with Jim.

" You will put this man in my bed," said Aunt Angelina Ann, as they puffed and panted over the lifting of Jim.

" Couldn't they both go in one bed ? " asked Sue. Serge had been put into the room usually occupied by her father and mother, and it seemed to her that it would be less trouble to have both men in one room.

" Oh no, it would never do," said the old lady. She

was stout, and she was slow, but she had sound common sense. " This poor man has a broken leg.   Think of the torture to him of having some one turning and twisting close to him."

" But you won't have a bed, Auntie."   There was trouble in Nell's tone as she spoke.   She and Sue slept on narrow, home-made cots, very hard and uncomfortable for any one as big and stout as the old aunt.

Aunt Angelina Ann laughed in her jolly fashion as she answered—

" I do not think there will be much question of sleeping at night for me just at present ; there will be some nursing to be done with such a pair of bashed-up creatures.   Poor fellows, how they must have suffered ! "

" Oh, it might have been worse, Auntie," said Jim as he was laid on the old lady's bed.   " I'm grateful to you for this bed, and I won't keep it a day longer than I can help."

" Ah, I believe that," and the old lady's big sides shook with laughter.   " There used to be a riddle that my mother used to ask, about what it was that every one wished to have, but no one wished to keep, and the answer was a bed.   Very good, wasn't it ?   Ha, ha, ha ! "   The old lady went off in a little gale of laughter, and, suffering as he was, Jim had to laugh too.

" I am going to phone for the doctor," said Nell, slipping down from the bed on which she had been standing to be able to lift Jim more easily.

" You can't phone—the wire is down," replied the old lady.   " We are just cut off, and we have got to put up with it.   Do you and Sue go and get into dry clothes, and then look after the old horse.   No, we

can't get a doctor to-day ; neither of you is fit for
the seven miles to Lupton, and the old horse isn't fit
either. I will lay this poor leg as straight as I can
get it, and will tie a broomstick to it to keep it so, and
when I have got him settled I will look after the other
poor fellow. Poor things, poor things ; but it would
have been worse for them if you two hadn't been so
spry in going to their help, so they will just have to
make the best of it. Now clear out, both of you, and
take care of yourselves ; I can manage."

And manage she did, in a cool, efficient way, that
made poor Jim Peters marvel as he lay on her bed
biting his tongue to keep back his groans, while her
big soft hands busied themselves with his broken
limb. The torture was over at last, and he could lie
still and rest, his senses dulled to drowsiness by fatigue
and by some weird concoction made of herbs and
administered scalding hot. It was awful to the taste,
and he had flatly refused, after the first mouthful, to
take any more ; but she told him in her quietly deter-
mined way that if he did not drink the whole lot
straight off she would pinch his nose and pour it down,
so he screwed up his courage and swallowed the potion
to escape the indignity of being treated like a baby or
a puppy.

He had his reward. In less than five minutes he
was fast asleep, and he lay like a log for hours and
hours. The other man, Serge Dobbin, appeared to be
in a very poor way indeed. Aunt Angelina Ann shook
her head a good bit as she worked away, shifting him
as best she could to get off his sodden clothes. Then
she put hot bottles to his feet and left him, going to
see that the girls were all right. Both Nell and Sue

were stretched on their narrow little beds, and both were asleep—just worn out by all they had gone through.

"Poor lambs!" murmured the old lady, and then she softly drew the curtain over the one small window for fear lest the daylight should waken the sleepers.

Matters in the kitchen claimed her attention for a time, then remembering her worry about the man Serge, she peeped in at the door of the bedroom to see whether he was looking more natural.

To her amazement the bed was empty, and he was not in the room. She made quite sure of this by going round to the other side of the bed just to see whether he had rolled off on the floor. Then she noticed that the door into her own room stood ajar, and, moving towards it with her slow, soft step, she pushed it a little wider and looked in.

Serge was bending over the bed; he had stripped the bedclothes from Jim and was fumbling with the thick vest Jim wore and which Aunt Angelina Ann had not deemed it necessary to remove, but she had bound a big towel round Jim's hips over the vest to hold the broomstick in place so that his broken leg should not shift. Serge was tugging and twisting to get this unfastened, and at the sight the old lady cried out indignantly—

"Here, stop that! Stop that, I say! What do you mean by coming in here interfering with Jim after I have put his leg comfortable?"

The man twisted round, craven fear in his eyes and an ugly scowl on his face.

"You trussed him up too tight, poor old Jim," he snarled. "Cried out, he did, and groaned, so I come in to see what was wrong with him. It don't do to hurt a man as knocked about as poor Jim."

For answer Aunt Angelina Ann stepped across the floor of that small room with quite surprising agility, and with her big soft hand she fetched Serge a resounding smack on the face. "Now get out and leave Jim alone." Her tone was quiet, but she towered above him with her big bulk, and she looked so equal to knocking him down and sitting upon him, that he shrank away, leaning weakly against the wall while he tried to justify himself.

"No use to get so rattled with me, old dame. I was only trying to help old Jim, poor fellow," he said with a whine in his tone that was meant to imply friendship, but only inspired distrust.

"Well, you will help him most by leaving him alone," said the old lady, and she fairly drove him into the next room, saw him get into bed, and coming out, slipped the very useful bolt which was on her side of the door. "He will have to come round by way of the kitchen if he wants to get in here again," she muttered with a chuckle, then bent anxiously over Jim to make sure that his bandage had not been shifted. She even slipped her hand down under his vest, and, withdrawing it, gave a satisfied nod, having made sure that what was there had not been removed.

CHAPTER IV

AN ANXIOUS NIGHT

AFTER two hours of sleep Nell awoke, feeling rather stiff, it is true, but otherwise not much the worse for her experiences in the rescue of the two men. She wanted to start off for Lupton then, so that a doctor might be fetched for the man with the broken leg.

" No, dearie, I don't want you to go to-night, and I'll tell you why." As she spoke, Aunt Angelina Ann drew Nell outside the kitchen door, but stood where she could keep a watchful eye on the door that led into the room where Serge Dobbin was in bed. " The fact is I had a bit of a scare while you were asleep, and I'm that much of a coward I don't want to be left with only Sue for the night. If you did not find the doctor at home, you see, you would have to stay in the town until morning."

" What frightened you ? " demanded Nell in surprise, for the old aunt was not by any means a nervous person in an ordinary way.

" That man in yonder, who calls himself Serge Dobbin," answered Aunt Angelina Ann, nodding in the direction of the bedroom door. " A regular bad lot he is, or my name is not Angelina Ann Draycot. I found him in my bedroom trying to unfasten the

bandages I had wound round Jim Peters to keep that
broomstick in its place. Trying to steal something
from the poor fellow he was, the scum that he is ! "

" Was there anything to steal ? " asked Nell in
surprise.

" I think so." The stout woman had dropped her
voice to a husky whisper now, and she towered over
Nell so that the whisper should not go any farther.
" Jim has a belt round his waist under his clothes, one
of those belts with pockets in it, and there are pearls
in the pockets, I should say by the feel. It was those
pearls Serge was trying to steal, and he would maybe
have had them if I had not happened along just right."

" Oh, Auntie, what shall we do ? " asked Nell, bleak
trouble showing on her face.

" We can't do anything for the moment except to
keep a sharp eye on Serge," the stout woman answered,
nodding her head. " You see now why I don't want
you to go to Lupton to-night. I don't think we need
worry about Jim's leg either, for it does not show any
sign of swelling, which is good, and it won't be serious
to leave it as it is for a few hours longer—not half so
serious as for the poor fellow to have half his savings,
or perhaps the whole of them, pinched by that mean
little skunk, Serge Dobbin."

" The boat that was wrecked, *The Bandalina Star*,
could not have come all the way from the pearling
grounds ! " cried Nell in surprise. " Why, it is more
than eight hundred miles from New Zealand to Australia, and think of the heavy seas she would have to
encounter. She looked only like a coaster."

" A coaster she most likely was," Aunt Angelina
Ann nodded wisely. " Very likely Jim Peters came

on another boat to Auckland, and then started to work his way on a coaster to some place round the coast that he wanted to reach. He might even have been making for New Plymouth. I will ask him when he wakes. He was too done to tell me anything when I was getting him comfortable."

" I wish Ned was at home, then we could have sent him for the doctor, and I should not have had to go away." Nell looked as bothered as she felt, but Aunt Angelina Ann patted her on the arm, saying in a soothing tone—

" Now, don't you worry ; we'll be all right. Ned will be home to-morrow evening, and though he will be tired with the long walk from Blackwell, he will be one more about the place. We have only to get through to-night, and then we shall have nothing to worry about."

Nell shook her head rather doubtfully. She had a shivering horror of a thief, and her aunt had said that Serge was trying to steal from his companion in disaster, so he must be a thief of an extra bad sort. But they would have to make the best of it for this night at least.

She had to go out of doors to milk the cows, and feed the poultry and the pigs; she had even to go the round of the sheep. In an ordinary way Sue would have helped her in these things, but plainly Aunt Angelina Ann must not be left in the house alone, so Nell slipped into the bedroom to give Sue a quiet word of warning. Then she started on the outdoor work with a determination to put it through with all possible dispatch.

When she went out to the edge of the cliff on her way

to count the sheep, she saw that the tide was full, and only the top of a mast sticking up through the grey, heaving water showed where *The Bandalina Star* lay fast gripped on the cruel black rocks which had been her doom.

Nell shivered violently, thinking of what would have been the fate of the two men if she and Sue had not been able to help them. She went round the sheep in a great hurry, and getting back gave the old horse an extra generous supper just by way of showing her gratitude for the help the creature had been in pulling the cart, with Jim Peters in it, from the wreck.

" That poor man, Jim Peters, has come awake, and he does not know where he is nor what he is saying,'' cried Sue, coming running out of the door to meet Nell as she came round from the stable when her work was done.

" Oh, I am sorry,'' replied Nell, who felt as if this was the last straw to their burden. " But it is really not wonderful that he should go off his head, seeing what he has had to bear to-day. I will go in and see if I can help Auntie with him.''

" Oh, Nell, won't you be scared ? '' cried Sue, shrinking visibly. " I ran away from the room when I heard him—he was screaming out that he must get to New Plymouth to-night or he would be too late.''

" Too late for what ? '' asked Nell, who was washing her hands with great energy at the little sink that was just behind the kitchen door.

" I don't know—I ran away,'' replied Sue with another shrug.

Staying only to half dry her hands, Nell went through the kitchen and entered the bedroom, where Aunt

Angelina Ann was vainly trying to soothe Jim Peters, who, sitting up in bed, was talking very fast, while the red flush on his cheeks, and the fever light in his eyes, showed how very ill he was.

" It is like this, old lady," he was saying to Aunt Angelina Ann, " I must be in New Plymouth to-morrow morning. If I cannot be there by the time the banks open, then David Draycot will be ruined, and the truest friend a man ever had will be put to shame by the man he helped. I must be there, I tell you—I must."

" Very well. You just lie down and take it quiet, while we see about the best means of getting you there." Aunt Angelina Ann spoke in a comfortable, soothing tone, which had its due effect on the poor fellow in his raging delirium. He stared wildly at her, muttering something they could not understand, and then he sank back on his pillow looking very spent.

" Auntie, what does he mean ? " asked Nell in a frightened whisper. " Is it our David he is talking about ? "

" I am afraid it is," replied Aunt Angelina Ann, and now her plump and kindly face was creased with care and fear. " It seems to me that David must have stood surety for this man, or something of the sort. The time is up to-morrow, and David will have to pay up or go to prison—that is what I have gathered from his talk. I hope I am mistaken, but it is plain there is big trouble of some sort."

" I've got the money right enough, or at least the money's worth," burst out the excited voice of the man on the bed. " That biggest pearl would more than cover the bank loan, and then there are all the others. Oh, but I must get to New Plymouth, do you hear, old lady? I must be at New Plymouth when bank opens to-morrow morning, or they will come on David to pay."

" And David is ill ! " exclaimed Nell in a tragic tone. "Oh, Auntie, what shall we do ? "

" We can't do anything to-night, that is certain," said the stout woman. " Perhaps when morning comes we shall see what is the best thing for us to do. Poor David ! I expect it is this business that has broken him down."

" If we could only let him know that things are going to be all right ! " cried Nell, who was suddenly in the grip of black depression. "Oh, Auntie, I don't feel as if I could wait until morning. Do you think I could run over to Scarth Point to-night ? The Judsons would let me use their phone, and I could call up New Plymouth, and say it was all right about the money."

" I could not have you going to Scarth Point alone to-night, I really could not," said Aunt Angelina Ann in great distress. " It is a good four miles there, even if you take short cuts, and they are dangerous on a dark night. Besides, there have been sheep-stealers in the district just lately, and they may still be operating up on the hills among the scattered flocks. Suppose you met any men of that sort. I should have no peace at all, I should just go wild with panic on your account. No, no, we have just got to stick things until morning."

" It is David I am thinking about," said Nell with quivering lips.

As a family the Draycots were very fond of each

other, and Nell was especially chummy with Dave, while Sue and Ned hung together in everything.

" It is David I am thinking about too," Aunt Angelina Ann said with a sigh.   " Poor lad, it is hard to have to suffer for being kind-hearted.   But perhaps it will impress the wisdom of the Bible on him."

" What has the Bible got to do with it ? " asked Nell in surprise, quite unable to see any connection between David's trouble and the Holy Scriptures.

Aunt Angelina Ann laughed softly, then said in her comfortable voice, " You would know what the Bible had to do with it if ever you had read the book of Proverbs very much.   However, I make no doubt that things will come right for David ; and as we can't do anything just now to make them come right, we have just got to wait patiently and make the best of things.   Now do you go and get your supper, and then come back here ; we won't leave the poor fellow alone, for fear that he may throw himself out of bed now he is off his head."

Nell did as she was told.   Furiously hungry she was, and the supper which Sue was cooking smelled very good indeed.   But she did not linger over her meal, for her aunt must be hungry too ; moreover, some supper must be carried to Serge, and neither Nell nor Sue fancied doing that bit.

Jim was lying quite quiet when she went back to the bedroom, and Aunt Angelina Ann was nodding sleepily in the big chair by the bed.

" You poor dear, you are nearly worn out with so much work and nursing," said Nell, as she put out her hand to help the stout woman out of the chair.

" Oh, there is a little go left in me yet," answered

Aunt Angelina Ann with her jolly laugh. " Just call me
if Jim wakes up excited at all. I do hope he will have
a quiet night, but I am no way sure that he will."

Nell groaned a little under her breath. In spite of
the sleep she had had in the day, she was feeling that
she would be quite ready to go to bed when bedtime
came ; but of course if Jim was going to be delirious,
then she must stay and help to nurse him, for in such
a case she could not leave her aunt to face things alone.

He was stirring gently with his hands under the bedclothes, but his eyes were shut and he looked very
peaceful ; perhaps it was all right. Anyhow she did
not mean to call her aunt unless there was serious need.
She sat down in the big chair where her aunt had been
resting, and her thoughts were at once busy with her
brother sick at New Plymouth. It was so dreadful
to think of David ill ; and if what this stranger had said
in his delirium was true, then David must also be in
grave anxiety, which, to Nell's way of thinking, was
worse than being sick in body. Oh dear, oh dear,
what a tangle it all was ! She heaved an impatient
sigh, thinking regretfully of the quiet monotony of
days that were gone, when there was no trouble anywhere, only constant hard work, very few holidays,
and not much money with which to buy things that
were necessary or desirable, or both.

" Are you there, Missy ? " asked a voice so close to
her that she started up in great surprise, thinking that
some one had come into the room and was speaking
to her ; but it was only Jim Peters, who had opened his
eyes and was looking at her with something so imploring in the quality of his gaze that she made haste
to stoop over him, asking what it was that he wanted.

She was not afraid of him, for he looked quite all right, and, besides, she could hear Aunt Angelina Ann talking to Serge in the next room. There was only the bolted door between them, and if need arose she could quickly draw that bolt and her aunt would be there to help her in a moment.

"Is there no one here but you?" he asked feebly, and he looked so white and spent that her heart ached for him.

"Auntie is in the next room," she said encouragingly. "Do you want her? I will call her and she will be here directly."

"I don't want her," he broke in hurriedly; "I wanted to get a chance to speak to you alone. I know I can trust you because you saved my life at the risk of your own. I have got some very valuable pearls on me—I was on my way to New Plymouth to lodge them in the Southern Bank. A man stood surety for me to get an outfit, and to pay my share when I went out in an Auckland boat. If I let that man down I shall never get over it. I am desperately afraid that the pearls will be stolen from me. That man, Serge Dobbin, suspects that I am carrying wealth, and he is always nosing round my things in the effort to find out. I have managed to get my belt undone, and I want you to take it and wear it yourself until I am able to look after it again." As he spoke Jim drew a wash-leather belt from under the bedclothes and held it out to Nell. "Take it quick, before any one comes. I shall not have a minute's peace if it is still on me. I had a horrid dream that Serge crept in while I was asleep, and was trying to get it from me."

"I would rather not take it, really I wouldn't," said

CHAPTER V

NELL ARRIVES AT SCARTH POINT

NELL sat up on her bed, she pushed back the clothes, and staring at Sue tried hard to get a grip of things, but she was still so dazed with her heavy sleep that she could not remember what had happened yesterday.

"Oh, Nell, do try and wake up quickly." Sue's voice was distinctly pettish, for she was in a hurry, and Nell really did look fearfully stupid. "Aunt Angelina Ann is so tuckered out that I want to get breakfast for her as soon as I can, but she is in such a hurry to get the doctor here that she says she will have no peace at all until you have started for Scarth Point."

Nell was awake now. She slipped from the bed and stood for a moment swaying dizzily. How horrid that the room would keep turning round in such an uncanny fashion, and the floor seemed heaving up to touch the ceiling. She staggered across to the wash-basin, and dipping her face in cold water immediately began to feel better.

"All right, Suey, I'll be off in two ticks," she said, reaching for a hairbrush and starting on a vigorous brushing of her hair. She was saying to herself that it was good she had not undressed last night, because she would be the quicker in starting for Scarth Point.

"You won't go until you have had your breakfast?"

cried out Sue, with a sound of dismay in her voice. Scarth Point was such a long way off, and Nell had not had much supper last night.

" I am going to start now, unless you would like me to stop and do the milking first," replied Nell. " I shall be nearly an hour and a quarter getting there, because the way is so rough, and I must be early to phone to Lupton before the doctor starts on his morning round."

" I can milk," said Sue valiantly, although in her heart of hearts she knew that she was scared stiff at the prospect ; for Spotty had a way of kicking viciously, while Fussy was so hard to milk that it nearly pulled her wrists out.

" I know you can," said Nell ; " but I hate for you to do it, because I know that you are afraid of Spotty. Just tie her leg to the post, and then she cannot damage you, nor yet put her foot in the bucket."

" I had not thought of tying her leg to the post ; what a brainy idea ! " cried Sue, who was making the fire in the kitchen stove. " If you won't wait for breakfast, Nell, at least take a bit of bread in your hand. You will faint with hunger before you get to Mrs. Judson's house, and you can't go marching in demanding a breakfast straight off."

" I will get a bit of bread," said Nell, making a dive for the breadpan in the corner ; then drawing a rather battered felt hat down over her curly bobbed hair, she called out a brisk " So long, Suey, old thing ; keep your end up, I will be back as soon as I can."

" So long, Nell ; don't run your legs off, I can manage all right," Sue called back ; and then Nell was gone, sloping across the paddock at the back, to take the standing on the threshold, her hair rough, her face streaked as if with crying, and her clothes so creased and crumpled that at the first glance Nell knew they had not been taken off last night.

" Nell Draycot, how truly good of you to come ! " cried Mrs. Judson, stretching out her hands in welcome, while a sob caught at her throat. " Oh, I was praying all day yesterday that God would send some one to help me, and now you have come."

" What is the matter ? " asked Nell, and in the face of fresh calamity she suddenly found her strength coming back to her.

" Ben had a fall when he was trying to mend the corner of the barn where the gale had stripped the roofing," answered Mrs. Judson, drawing Nell into the house, and pushing her down into the chair standing by the unlighted stove. " The gale broke our wire down too, and I should have come over yesterday to get you to phone for the doctor, but Ben has hurt his left hand and his right arm ; he has sprained his ankle too, and he could not lift baby from the cradle, nor look after Eddie, so I could not leave. I just had to wait for some one to come along, but not a soul came near. Oh, it is dreadful to live in these out-of-the-way places ! "

" It is a bit awkward when there is trouble," admitted Nell, who was leaning back in the chair, and feeling better because she could sit still for a minute or two ; then the comic side of the situation came uppermost, and she began to laugh softly.

" Where does the joke come in ? " demanded Mrs. Judson in a rather sour tone. She had started to rake out the ashes from the stove, and she clattered the poker violently, for she thought Nell was making fun of her.

" I was thinking that at least we are spared the bother of having to constantly answer the door to callers, and tradesmen, and beggars," Nell answered, then leaned back in the chair and laughed and laughed ; because if she had not laughed she would certainly have cried, and merriment seemed better than tears.

Mrs. Judson stood with the poker in her hand, staring at Nell, her face screwed into a pucker of disapproval at such levity ; then somehow the comical side of the situation appealed to her also, and, sitting down in the chair on the other side of the stove, she began to laugh too.

At the sound of so much mirth, the elder child, a mischievous imp of three called Eddie, came running out of the bedroom in his nightgown to join in the sport, while the baby left off crying, and the deep voice of Ben Judson was heard calling out an inquiry as to what they were laughing about.

" We are not laughing about anything," called back his wife. " I mean there is nothing to laugh about, only if we don't laugh we shall cry, so laughing seems best."

" Just like a woman," growled the deep voice of Ben Judson ; then to the surprise of his wife and Nell, he began to laugh also, while young Eddie fairly shrieked with glee, dashing back into the bedroom, eager to be with a daddy who could laugh.

" Mr. Judson is not very bad if he can laugh like that," said Nell, desiring to comfort the anxious woman.

" Oh, it is the laughing that will do him good,"

panted Mrs. Judson, who was out of breath from so much merriment. " I declare I feel better myself. Before you came I did not feel that I had another kick left in me; fairly tuckered out I was. But the sight of you, and the sound of your laughing, has made me feel like a different person. I'll make haste and get this fire going so that I can cook breakfast; you will be ready for another by this time, I guess."

" Oh, I have not had any breakfast yet, only a bit of bread in my hand that I munched as I came along," said Nell; " I am nearly hungry enough to eat my boots. While you are getting breakfast I can go and let out the poultry and pigs; shall I ? "

" You are a kind girl ! " cried Mrs. Judson, while from his bed in the other room Ben Judson called out to her to tell her where to find the breakfast for the hungry animals.

" Do you think you would milk for me ? " asked Mrs. Judson, with an imploring note in her voice. " I did it last night, but I am so afraid of cows. Why, even Eddie is not such a coward as I am."

" Eddie likes de moos," said the small boy, flourishing his arms, and then he ran to bring the milk bucket for Nell, and to show her where to find the stool.

" Take a cup with you, Nell, and have a drink of milk warm from the cow; it will help you hold out until breakfast is ready," said Mrs. Judson; and Nell was thankful for the suggestion, for she seemed to have no strength left, and the tears staved off by laughter hung perilously near at hand.

Eddie, in his little striped pink nightgown, came running out to the barn with her. It was a good thing the morning was warm and that the ground was dry, for he was barefoot. He was quite useful too, for he showed Nell the little trap door which fastened back to let the ducks out of their pen, and he fetched the tin bucket of corn for the fowls, jabbering all the time of the things he did, and the way in which he helped daddy.

Nell sat down on the stool beside a red and white cow, and tucking her head into the creature's warm side set to work to milk her. Luckily she was a peaceable animal, who did not mind the hands of a stranger on her udder, so Nell found the work go easily. She had a cup of milk, and immediately began to feel better. She gave Eddie some milk too, and, carrying her full bucket of milk to the house, came back to start on the next cow. But this was a fidgety beast, and she had her work cut out to get the milk without having the bucket kicked over. This way and that swayed the cow, until finally Nell had to force her against the fence and rope her there. All this hindered her of course, and by the time she was through with feeding the creatures and milking, Mrs. Judson had got a really sumptuous breakfast cooked.

There was corn porridge and milk—plenty of milk ; there was tea, sweet and strong, with scrambled eggs, and toast and butter. Nell was fairly ashamed of her appetite, but Mrs. Judson kept insisting on her having a little bit more, and just a fragment after that, until at last she simply could not swallow another mouthful.

"Now, I will start for Lupton and the doctor," she said, pushing back her chair and feeling at peace with the world once more and ready to face anything.

"You can't go all that way!" cried Mrs. Judson, aghast. "I should say it is over eleven miles from here to Lupton, and you have done four already."

" I shall manage it, don't you worry," Nell answered cheerfully. " Of course I shall be late getting there, and the doctor will be off no one knows where, but it is the only thing to do. We want him so badly at our house, and you want him too. Would you mind if he comes to us first ? If I find him, that is. You see that poor man, Jim Peters, is so very ill, and it is so bad that his broken leg should have to wait so long to be set."

" Of course you must have him first," said Mrs. Judson. " Ben has no bones broken, though he is gashed and bruised in all directions, and his ankle is very painful. We are so grateful to you for coming, and for all that you have done for us. A good, kind girl you have been. I only wish we had a horse for you to ride, but we haven't a nag on the place except the two colts, and they are away in the far paddock. I expect it would take the best part of the day to catch them, and then they are only half broken. You see we have lent old Twister to Jack Rudd this week, and that has made the trouble. If the old horse had been at home I could have harnessed it to the cart and driven both the children into Lupton yesterday, to tell the doctor we wanted him."

" I can do the walk," said Nell valiantly ; and indeed, fortified as she was by her bountiful breakfast, it did not seem such a very impossible task to tramp eleven miles, though the day was hot and the road was rough.

" Why don't you go over to Jack Rudd's place ? " said Mrs. Judson. " That is only five miles from here. It is inland, too, so his wire is not likely to be down."

" I might do that," said Nell, getting on to her

feet and reaching for her hat, which she had taken off when she sat down to breakfast.

It was with her right hand she reached for her hat ; with her left she, at that moment, felt a hard little knob somewhere under her jersey, and she nearly cried out with astonishment and dismay as she remembered that Jim Peters's belt was strapped round her waist under the woollen jersey, and in the pockets of the belt were those pearls which Serge Dobbin was so anxious to steal.

" I think I will go to Lupton," she said, trying to look as if she had not had a shock. " I shall be sure of getting the doctor if I go there."

But the thing she was saying to herself as she turned away from the table was that there was a branch of the Southern Bank at Lupton, and she could carry the pearls there and deposit them in the name of Jim Peters.

CHAPTER VI

NELL CHANGES HER PLAN

' Now, which of these tracks do I take, I wonder ? "
As Nell asked her question she gazed uncertainly first
to the right and then to the left where the track
forked. The trouble was she had no very good sense
of direction. Mrs. Judson had told her to veer to the
left on the top of the hill, and that had been easy
enough, for when she had been on the hills she could,
when looking back, get a glimpse of the sea shining
far away to the edge of the horizon ; but now she was
down on lower ground she was in a bewildering laby-
rinth of ti-tree scrub, and there were cattle-tracks to
the left and to the right, until she became so confused
she could not decide which was the proper track that
she had to follow, and which were the tracks made by
the wandering feet of grazing cattle and sheep.

She was very tired, too, and so hot that she did not
know how to walk. According to her reckoning she
had done about seven miles, and so had about four
more to go.

" I will take my jersey off and carry it," she said to
herself, then suddenly remembered the belt that was
fastened underneath, over her cotton frock, and
decided that she would leave the jersey where it was,

even though she might be fainting with heat and dripping with perspiration.

" I could fasten it round under my frock, but I don't think I will," she murmured to herself, as she walked slowly along ; but the heat was so great that at last she could bear it no longer, and, coming to a pause under a stunted tree that gave a little shade, she dragged off the thick woollen jersey and, unfastening the belt, lifted the skirt of her cotton frock and strapped the belt on underneath. Now it showed more, for the cotton stuff was so thin. She turned her head this way and that, trying to get a better view of herself.

" It does hump out a bit here and there, but of course no one would know what it was I was carrying there," she murmured uneasily, and a cold little shiver shook her at the thought of the wealth she carried. Oh, why had she not remembered that she was wearing the belt and taken it off before she left home ? Yet perhaps it was better that she had it, for supposing she had hidden it somewhere at home, and that fearful man, Serge Dobbin, had found it. Then all chance of Jim Peters being able to pay his debt to David would be gone. The bare thought made Nell cower and shrink. What was it that Jim Peters had said ? Failing payment, the man who had helped him might have to go to prison. How awful to think of poor old David in prison, and that for no fault of his own, but just because he had tried to help a needy man.

Carrying her jersey over her arm, Nell pressed forward at a brisk pace. She was so much cooler now that walking was quite a pleasure. Indeed she would have felt almost festive if only she could have been quite absolutely sure that she was on the right road ;

but she was not sure, and so a chill little doubt was keeping her company all the way and marring her peace.

On, and on, and on she tramped. She had left the ti-tree scrub far behind, and she was walking across wide grassy valleys, and toiling up long slopes to reach the top of the hill, and then to go down on the other side. But never a human being did she see, and although she was following a track of a sort, she could not be really sure that it was the track to the town, or merely a way made by the passing of sheep and cattle.

She marched up yet another hill, this one higher than the others. When she reached the top great was her joy to see a difference in the view outspread before her. She could see cultivated land ; her joyful gaze took note of telephone posts ; there was a grove of trees quite near—yes, and she could see a house ! That was surely a road running yonder, and far away in the distance she made out a huddle of houses that must be Lupton.

It was very far away. Something like dismay came into her heart as she realized how many miles she must have walked through missing the right way, for now she could see that she was back on the road from her own home to Lupton. If she had only taken the right track she would have been in Lupton long before this—of course she would. Perhaps she would have found the doctor and have been riding back with him. How glad she would be to ride. Her feet were dreadfully tired. In fact, she was so tired all over that it seemed to her she simply could not walk any farther, and Lupton was still such a long distance away.

She went down the hill rather slowly. She would

strike the road to Lupton about a mile farther on—at least she hoped so; meanwhile she had to skirt some cultivated ground and pass through a grove of tall trees.

Before she reached the trees she encountered a big herd of cattle feeding, but she took no especial notice of them; growing up on a farm she was not afraid of cattle, and probably if she took no notice of them they would take no notice of her.

She was limping a little now, one foot was getting sore, and there was still quite a long way to go. A thudding of hoofs and a snorting of breath close behind caused her to turn quickly, and then to her dismay she saw that a big bull had detached himself from the herd and was coming after her.

" You won't catch me, with luck," she cried, and then was away like the wind. How she ran! Her sore foot was forgotten; she did not remember how tired she was; the only thing which concerned her was how she could get away from the big beast that was chasing her. With unerring instinct she was heading for the trees. If only there had been a fence anywhere in sight she would have made for that, but although it was cultivated land, so far as she could see there were no fences. If only she could reach the trees she could dodge round them until her enemy grew tired of trying to catch her. Nell had been chased by cattle before to-day, and was expert in the art of dodging, or she thought she was.

What a long way it seemed, and she was so dreadfully short of breath. There was a sharp pain in her side, too, and she really did not feel as if she could run any farther. But the bull was gaining on her, and she could hear the snorting breath getting closer and closer.

Panic seized her and she shot ahead, putting all her will-power into her going. The trees were close now. Very well; once she reached them she could twist and turn and dodge, and so gain time to get her breath back.

She passed the first tree so close that the bull in hot pursuit drove right into it with a force that sent it staggering. This gave Nell an advantage that enabled her to dart forward to where the trees grew thicker still. The bull recovered from the shock and was coming on again; Nell twisted sharply round three trees growing close together; she skirted some low bushes, and then—oh, joy !—she saw a tree that she could climb. One big trunk had partly fallen, it was leaning against two others, and it had tufty little branches sticking out from the main trunk.

Nell swung herself up among the scratching, tufty branches; she climbed until she was well above the reach of her enemy, and then coming to a place where she could sit comfortably, she settled down to wait until the bull forgot about her and went back to the herd.

Things do not always fall out according to expectation. To her disgust Nell found that instead of going back to the herd, the herd came wandering up to where their leader had gone. They were all in the grove now, fifty-seven of them, and the bull made fifty-eight. Some were feeding and some were lying down, but the bull, which was the cause of the trouble, was standing watchful beneath that sloping trunk up which she had climbed so nimbly.

Nell knew where she was now. In spite of all the

miles she had walked since leaving Scarth Point, she was still about two and a half miles from Lupton, and she was only about four and a half miles from her own home. How dreadful to have failed every one like this! Poor Jim Peters so ill, and in such need of the doctor. Ben Judson needing a doctor too, and she who had set out to bring them help, and had walked so far to do it, was sitting up a tree like a scared kitten, while the cattle down below looked as if they might stay in the shade of those trees all day.

"It is fearfully bothering, but it would have been worse for me—oh, so very much worse—if there had been no tree that I could climb," muttered Nell to herself as she leaned at ease against the tufty branches and chuckled over her really good fortune.

The track to the town passed through the grove. Nell told herself that some one would surely come along presently. She could call out to them and tell them how she was treed, and so the cattle would be driven away, and she would be set free. She might even get a lift into Lupton, or the somebody who was going to rescue her might carry the message for the doctor, and she could go straight back home.

Meanwhile there was nothing to do but wait. Nell decided that there were worse places in which to wait than the sloping trunk of a tree that had tufty branches. She was quite comfortable on her perch; she had drawn her jumper over her head again, and she was pleasantly warm even though a cool breeze stole through the trees.

An hour she must have sat there, and the afternoon was getting on. She had eaten some of the food Mrs. Judson had insisted on packing for her journey, but she had a raging thirst and decided that she did not want any more to eat until she could get some water to drink. Her great trouble was that she was so sleepy, and she knew that it would never do for her to fall asleep on her perch or she might tumble off to drop down in the midst of the cattle that were still grouped down below.

If only some one would come ! Another hour passed away ; the cattle were a bit farther away now, and the big bull had ceased to be watchful. Nell told herself that at this rate in about another hour they would be far enough away for her to make a bolt for it. The trouble was that it was so far to a fence. The track through the grove was not a proper highroad, but was the nearest—and indeed the only—way to Lupton from the outlying farms on that part of the coast.

Wheels at last ! Nell could have shouted with delight, especially as the vehicle, whatever it was, came from the coast and was going in the direction of Lupton. She would get a ride—how good ! Her courage sank a little as she reflected that even if she rode into Lupton she might have to walk back and again run the gauntlet of the cattle ; but perhaps the doctor would bring her back. No use to cross the bridge until she got to it. She peered through the screen of branches in which she was half-hidden. A cart, drawn by a grey horse, was coming ; two men were sitting in the cart. She was just going to open her mouth to shout and ask them to stop, when something familiar and sinister in the appearance of the man sitting beside the driver caught her attention and silenced her as effectually as if a gag had been thrust into her mouth. For the man was Serge Dobbin !

She was sure it was Serge, and if her eyes had needed any further confirmation it came to her then in the raised voice of the man talking to the driver, who appeared to be an old acquaintance.

" Spotted where he carried them, I did, and I should have got them all right enough if it hadn't been for the old woman." The high-pitched voice of Serge carried well, and the words came clearly to Nell, who was now cowering in the little thicket of tufty branches, chiefly concerned with remaining undiscovered by the two in the cart, which was coming so slowly towards the tree in which she was perched.

The driver made some answer which she could not catch, for his voice was deep and low, and then the voice of Serge went on again—

" The old woman was asleep, and I had another try. They were gone, and I am sure the gal has got them. When I heard she had gone for the doctor I just slipped out and followed, for miss knows where them pearls is hid, and it is miss I am looking to find."

Nell gave a sharp little gasp, and buried her head low among the scratchy branches. Would either of the men look up, she wondered ; would they see her foot poking out ? Oh, if for ten minutes—if for five minutes even, she could get an invisible cloak in which to wrap herself so that she might be hidden from those men down below ! If only she could !

The cart was passing her tree ; the driver had laid his whip lightly across the flanks of his horse to make it move more quickly, and the voice of Serge, vibrant and rasping, floated up to her.

" Twenty thousand pounds' worth, so I was told, for there are two dozen so much alike in size and colour that they might be the same one for all that any ordinary person could tell. No, I have not seen them. I don't know that Jim ever guessed that I knew, but I did, and that was why I shipped on *The Bandalina Star* with him, looking for my chance. I should have had it too if it had not been for the old woman and for miss——"

They were out of hearing, the cart had passed underneath the tree, and the two men had not looked up. Truly their eyes had been holden, and she was safe—as safe as if she had been wrapped in that cloak which could render her invisible. For a few minutes Nell remained with her head pressed down in the tufty branches, sobbing quietly from sheer relief because of her escape. Then she suddenly twisted herself to a more upright position and started to think hard, very hard indeed. She could not see the cart now—the trees blocked the view of the track in that direction ; she could not hear it even, but she knew she must remain where she was for a little while longer yet.

When it was safe for her to get down, what was she to do ? It was not now possible for her to go on to Lupton for the doctor, for she would most probably encounter Serge, and then——

A shiver crept down her back. If those pearls were stolen, Jim could not pay his debt, and David would be ruined. She said it over again, as she had said it so many times to herself since she had heard poor Jim Peters raving in delirium. What could she do ? What could she do ?

" I can go straight to New Plymouth ; it is only

forty miles—no, it is not forty miles, it is only thirty-five miles. I remember father said the team could do it comfortably in two days, and I can do it in three days. I can, and I will."

She spoke aloud, and she spoke with immense decision. She had to keep her courage up, for the task in front of her was of the most daunting kind, and she felt her courage oozing out at her finger-tips.

Twenty thousand pounds! And she was wearing it in the belt strapped round her waist, under her poor cotton frock that was already torn and dirty from rough usage. It was the price of David's good name—yes, and of the good name of Jim Peters too. Well, she was going to do it somehow, and the whole success of her attempt would lie in her giving Lupton a very wide berth indeed.

She did not know the way to New Plymouth, but she knew it was by the sea, so she would follow the coast until she came to the town. Thirty-five miles, and her feet were so tired already.

" I am going to do it, I am," she murmured presently as she made her way slowly down from the tree, for the cattle had wandered over the hill and were out of sight.

" I am going to do it even if I have to crawl into New Plymouth on my hands and knees, for where there is a will there is mostly a way."

CHAPTER VII

HER BIG UNDERTAKING

NELL's first thought when she came down from the tree was where she could find water to drink. In an ordinary way she would have made straight for the house that she had seen from the top of the hill, and which was about half a mile farther away on the road to Lupton. Now, she could not go there—she could not. For aught she knew the driver of the cart and Serge Dobbin might have halted there on their way to the town ; they might even be there now.

What she had to do was to strike backward on her tracks until she came in sight of the sea, then she would go forward again, keeping the sea always in sight until she reached New Plymouth. With care the food she had left would last for that day, and to-morrow she would have to beg, for she had no money—not a penny piece. No, she would not beg, she would borrow. She would walk straight up to a house ; she would say, " I am on my way to New Plymouth to find my father and my mother. I want a meal, and I will pay you when I get home." Oh, it would all be quite easy ; the only thing was that she had to get as far away from Lupton as possible before she presented herself at any house, because if Serge Dobbin was looking for her, and found that she had not been seen in Lupton, he might easily start searching for her among the lone houses scattered here and there through that sparsely populated district.

She remembered having passed a little stream a few miles back. Well, as she had to go back until she was within sight of the sea, she would make for that stream. But she was so fearfully thirsty, and the miles were so long on that hot afternoon.

It was dogged determination that forced her onward. She had to make a wide circuit to avoid the cattle, and then she went forward, limping a little, but on the whole doing better than she had expected. Really and truly it was her fear of encountering Serge Dobbin that drove her along.

By the sun she judged it was quite late in the afternoon before she reached the stream, and by that time she was so fearfully tired that she could hardly drag one foot in front of the other.

Down on the ground she dropped, and, cupping her hand, she drank and drank until her thirst was gone. Oh, how good the water tasted !

A short rest, a little food, and another long drink, and then she was away again. That long rest in the tree had really done her good, and as the evening was cool and pleasant, she decided that she must walk as far as she could before darkness dropped, and she must sleep just in the place where night found her. The dread of night spent in the open was before her. She was always afraid of the dark. She and Sue mostly had a light in their bedroom at home just because they were nervous. But darkness in a safe little bedroom next door to father and mother was not to be compared with darkness out on a windy hillside, with queer little whispering noises all around. It would be dreadfully weird, and she would be so scared that sleep would be impossible, yet even that was better than that Serge Dobbin should have any chance of stealing the pearls which were the price of David's liberty, and of the good name of poor Jim Peters.

On, and on; she was walking along the crest of a ridge of hills now. Such high hills they were, and to her great content there was the sea away on her left, gleaming in the evening light. It would be dark in about another hour, but in an hour she might get a mile or two farther on her way, and every mile counted. She did not know how far she was from home, but thought it might be eleven or twelve miles. Only that little way, and she had been all day doing it. Her foot was not sore now; she had torn her handkerchief in half, and washing it in the stream at her last halting-place had put it over the sore place so that her shoe did not chafe it.

She wanted to reach some trees so that she might have just a little bit of shelter for the night. But so far as she could see there were no trees, only wide, grassy downs. Then presently, as she toiled up over another fold of the downland, she espied a little hut, very much in ruins, yet possessing a roof and a door. Evidently it had been built for the shelter of shepherds at some time in the remote past. To Nell it seemed a very haven of refuge when she reached it just before dark. She pulled an armful of dried grass, and spreading it on the earth floor of the shed she shut the door, pushed a big stone against it, and then lay down, thankful indeed that she had found a shelter. So tired she was that not even her condition, nor the thought of the dreadful worry on her account which they would be enduring at home, had any power to keep her awake. She just fell into slumber, and lay like a log for hours and hours.

Daylight was coming in at the window when she awoke. It was only a small window high up in the wall, a glassless opening that let in the fresh air.

Shivering with cold, stiff in all her limbs, and ravenously hungry, Nell scrambled to her feet, and, dragging away the stone, pulled open the door.

The sun was coming up over the hill, and its red beams were catching a reflection from the shining surface of the sea. It was going to be a fine day. A little sob of thankfulness struggled in Nell's throat. She was so wretchedly cold and miserable. The weight of the wealth she carried seemed to press in upon her very soul. It was not that the belt was heavy, it was the awful responsibility of safeguarding the pearls which seemed to press so heavily on her. She would have been so happy if she could have roamed those hills that morning free from care. To be out-of-doors, to be free to wander where she would, that constituted happiness for Nell.

She had saved one bit of crust for the morning, and standing in the doorway of the shepherd's hut, she devoured the dry bit of bread thinking nothing had ever tasted nicer, and wishing with all her heart that she had a bit four or five times as big. But it was better than nothing, indeed it was, and she went forward at a good pace, walking all the faster because she was so cold.

The sun mounted higher and poured its beams upon

her ; she became warm, then hot, and finally she had to pull off her jersey again. She hated doing this, because, to her fancy, the belt underneath showed so plainly. Carrying the jersey she went steadily forward. She could not even guess the mileage now. So hungry she was, and so tired, that every half-dozen steps were like a mile, and she was still going forward, taking a bee line across the hills, working through scrublands where the prickly growths were up to her knees. One or two distant farms she had seen, but she had given them a wide berth. She hoped to come upon a little house where the people would not be so likely to ask inconvenient questions. Then, too, at a little house there would not be likely to be so many dogs, and she was very much afraid of dogs. Most lone, out-lying farms had two or three big savage dogs always roaming at large, and these would certainly make a dash for any unfortunate person advancing on foot.

She had come to the end of the downland, and was having to make the circuit of an immense wheat-field, because she would not walk through the standing corn ; but she took her circuit on the side of the field that was nearest to the sea, it was her guide to her goal, and she might not wander away from the sight of it. At the end of the wheat came a long stretch of oats ; already these had the silvery gleam in the green that showed them ripening fast. But the oat-field was even bigger than the field of wheat, and by the time she had skirted that she was right out on the edge of the cliffs. She was faint and sick with hunger and weariness, and at first she thought that her sight was playing her false, for right away across a small bay

she could see tall chimneys, a huddle of houses, and a
cluster of shipping fringing the shore.

New Plymouth it was. She had been there once,
and she could not fail to remember the manner in
which the spit of land ran out to sea with the houses
clustering thickly upon it, and the shipping round the
shore. But it was so far away. How would she ever
reach it ? For a few minutes her courage wavered
and drooped. She could have sunk to the ground
where she stood, and cried and cried like a silly kid.
She could have done it, but she did not ; instead she
gabbled over and over again to herself, talking like a
parrot that has just learned some new words, " I have
got to get to New Plymouth as quickly as I can, and I
have to go to the Southern Bank for Jim Peters, and
that will save David from having to go to prison. I
can save David from having to go to prison. I can,
and I will ! "

Oh, brave words, and brave spirit behind them !
But it is possible that in spite of her determination
Nell would have sunk to the earth and lain there lack-
ing the strength and energy to rise, only at that moment
she espied a little house standing by itself farther on—
the sort of little house where there would not be likely
to be fierce dogs, and where she might beg a piece of
bread to keep her from starvation.

How far away it seemed. Black darkness came in
front of Nell and threatened to swallow her up. She
put out her hands as if to push it away, and walked
slowly forward. She was groping now like a blind
person, and stumbling from weakness as she went.
Then in her groping her hand encountered a gate. This
she pushed open, and resting against it for a minute

recovered a little, and saw that the door of the little house was only a few steps away.

Summoning all her energy she let go her hold of the gate, and walking to the door knocked.

No one came in answer to her summons, and when she had knocked three times, in sheer desperation she tried the door, which yielded to her touch. Pushing it open she found herself in a little room, poorly furnished but clean, and on the table the remains of a meal not cleared away. There was a wedge of meat pie still remaining on a dish, a piece of bread on a plate and some butter, while a coffee-pot, half full of rather muddy coffee, stood on a little tray at the end of the table.

" It looks like stealing, but it isn't, for father will pay for it," said Nell, speaking aloud but in a very waggly tone as she lurched across the room, then dropping into a chair drew the dish towards her and started to eat the bit of pie.

How good it was ! And the cold, muddy coffee was good too. She cleared off the pie, she ate most of the bread and butter, and she drained the coffee-pot to the dregs. Then, slipping on her jersey, she lay down on the hard little settee in front of the window and went to sleep at once. She had meant to keep awake so that she might give her explanations to the woman of the house who would come back to find that her place had been entered and raided. It was one thing to mean to keep awake, but quite another thing to do it. She was so very tired, and now that her hunger and thirst had been satisfied she was so absolutely comfortable, that she was asleep before she knew that she was even drowsy.

The hours passed, the flies buzzed in the window of

the little house, and Nell sighed gently in her sleep, but she did not rouse. The afternoon merged into evening, shadows gathered in the corners of that bare little room, and spread and spread until it was dark. But Nell slept on, utterly worn out by her great undertaking, and all that it had cost her in the way of hardship.

There was a highroad not far from the little house, but Nell had not seen it, for she had approached the house from the other side. Many times during the hours that Nell had lain asleep, motor-cars had passed along this road, heavy wagons had lumbered slowly past, and people on horseback had trotted smartly along. An hour or so after darkness had fallen, and when Nell's slumbers were growing less profound, there came a tremendous crash that roused her to wakefulness, and a shrill screaming that frightened her so much that she rolled off the hard little settee, thinking that the person who screamed must be in the house.

But the little room was empty except for herself. It was in heavy darkness too, and in her first bewildered awakening she could not remember where the door was.

"Oh, where am I, and what shall I do?" she cried, with a sense of panic brooding down upon her.

She could see the window now, because a red glow was making itself seen there. Gathering herself up from the floor on to which she had rolled, Nell peered out. She could see lights not far from the house, she could hear loud talking, and then another scream as of some one in dreadful pain. What could be happening out there in the dark? And where, oh, where was the door of the house?

Groping and groping, Nell made the circuit of the room. A door she found, and opened, but it did not lead out-of-doors ; and shutting it again, she passed on, groping her way round the room and racking her brain to remember what the room had looked like when she entered. But she had been so near to collapse then that she simply had not noticed it at all.

Ah, there was the door ! It was almost close to the window, only she had started from the other side, and so had been obliged to grope her way right round the room.

She groped for the handle and opened the door. How good to smell the sweet fresh air after the hot stuffiness of the little room. She drew a long breath of relief, and then started to where the lights were showing, so that she might find out what was wrong.

Men's voices were talking in loud tones. She heard one man shout to another, and the voices had such a sound of fear that she shivered and shivered, while her skin goose-fleshed in the most uncomfortable fashion as she went towards the lights.

" Why, there is a highroad here ! " she muttered in great surprise, and wondered that she had not noticed it when she approached the house from the other side. "And there has been a motor accident. I wonder if some one has been very badly hurt ? "

She was quite close to the road now, making her way through a little thicket of brush canes which hid her from view. She had somehow missed the path from the house to the road, and was stumbling her way across a patch of neglected garden ground. She was close enough now to see what had happened : a motor-car coming along the road had run into a timber tug heavily laden. The car seemed to be a pretty complete wreck, and from the talk of the men some one had been rather badly hurt. Nell was just going to call out and ask if she could help. She was just going to offer the hospitality of the little house which had sheltered her, when one of the men busy doing something amongst the wreckage of the car turned round to answer some question put to him by one of the others, the light of a lantern held high glared down in his face, and Nell choked back a cry of dismay, for the man was Serge Dobbin.

CHAPTER VIII

NED DRAYCOT was a snub-nosed, freckled boy of
twelve, and he came marching along the road to his
home, with his school bag on his back, whistling blithely
as he thought of the week-end in front of him. It
would be holidays in about two weeks now. But
holidays to a farmer's son on a New Zealand farm are
only another name for very hard work, especially the
summer holidays. Not that Ned minded hard work
when it was work for his arms and legs. What constituted hard work for him was swotting over books and
sums, learning about the past in order to fit himself
for the future, and doing bewildering things with
figures on paper. He endured the time at school for
the pleasure of the week-ends at home. He even tried
to work his honest best, although it was always a matter
of luck when his sums came right. He never understood them, nor saw any reason in them, and—well, he
fairly hated school work all round.

It was Friday evening, and until Monday morning
he need not look at a book nor think of a figure. He
would just go round with his father, helping with the
pigs, and counting the sheep. He could count sheep
better than Nell, who always got mixed and muddled

in counting a flock that ran into a hundred and fifty
or so.

Then the food at home was better than at the house
of Miss Penrose, where he lodged when he was attend-
ing school. Oh, it was grand to be going home, and he
whistled and sang, fetching out the echoes from the
hills, and beguiling the long miles with the noise he
was making.

Not that the way seemed very long. He was so
interested in things on the way—that corn on Houndle
Hill had changed a lot since last week; it was green
still, but a different green. There was rye on the
lower slope of Barrow Heights, and that had changed
too. Everything had taken a step forward. Harvest
would not be long now, and harvest was a jolly time.

Here he was at the lower gate already. This was
home, for now he was on his father's land, and he
looked round him with a pride of possession that
stirred him up to do his very best to help keep things
going.

" I'll just put my back into things to-morrow, then
father will say how glad he will be when I leave school,"
he muttered to himself, and started to whistle more
shrilly than before.

He was looking keenly for some glimpse of his
father, but there seemed to be no life at all about the
place—not human life, that is. The old horse was
feeding in the home paddock, and the cows were there
too. The sight of the cows brought a vague sense of
trouble to Ned. They should have been down by the
house now, being milked. They had not been milked,
that was easy to know from the fulness of their udders,
and going out of the straight track to the house, he

rounded up the cows, driving them home for milking. He said to himself that his father must be late afield to-night, and perhaps Nell and Sue were helping him, or the girls might be having a picnic down on the shore; only the thought of this made him twist his mouth into a grimace—he thought they might have waited for him to come home and join them.

He was not whistling now; he was looking very serious indeed as he drove the cows into the yard and fastened them up ready for milking. Then he went on to the house, reaching the back door just as Sue came out with the milk bucket.

" Hallo, Suey ! " he called blithely. " Rather late with the milking, aren't you ? Where is father ? "

" Oh, Ned, so you have come. How glad I am ! " cried Sue, letting the milk bucket fall with a crash, and running to hug Ned in a bearlike fashion.

" Here, steady on, old girl. Why this thusness ? " he asked, emerging from the hugging rather breathless and crumpled.

" Oh, Ned, we are in the most awful trouble ! " cried Sue, who was inclined to hysterics and exaggeration.

" What's up ? " demanded Ned, his tone still cheerful. But a grim look had crept into his face, and his eyes were anxious.

" Father and mother have been sent for to New Plymouth because David is ill," said Sue, tumbling her information out in a great hurry. " Then *The Bandalina Star* was wrecked on the Black Rocks, and we— that is, Nell and I—saved two men at the risk of our lives and brought them home. We could not get a doctor for them because our wire is down."

" I saw that as I came along," broke in Ned. " Nell and I will mend it to-morrow."

Sue gulped hard, choked back a sob, and went on : " You have not heard the worst yet. The man, Jim Peters, the one who has a broken leg, was on his way home from the pearling. He had a lot of pearls on him, in a belt round his waist, and they are gone. Aunt Angelina Ann is nearly off her head about it, because she says the other man, Serge Dobbin, has stolen them."

" Well, we can't help that," said Ned crossly. He was more taken aback than he would have cared to admit by this chapter of disasters, and, being dismayed, he at once became very cross.

" We can't help it, but it makes us pretty miserable all the same," said Sue. Then clutching at Ned again, she tucked her head down on his shoulder and broke into stormy crying.

" Here, stow it, Suey; stow it, I say ! " Ned's voice was loud and angry, but his face was pinched, and he was horribly frightened, for Sue always disdained tears, and had made such fun of Polly Mackarness only last week, because Polly had cried when she fell into a mud hole.

" Oh, Ned, I haven't told you all; there is more trouble yet, only I can't get it all out fast enough," wailed Sue, who was crying harder than ever, while her tears ran down inside Ned's collar, making him very damp and uncomfortable. That was the worst of girls, even nice ones like Sue : when they turned the water on they seemed to have no sense at all about turning it off again.

" Get it off your chest as fast as you can," urged

Ned, trying to wriggle himself in Sue's grip so that her tears did not run down his neck. Ugh, it was horrid !

" Jim Peters says that David lent him money to go pearling—no, did not lend it, he stood security ; is hat it ? "

" You mean Dave stood surety," said Ned, and now indeed he looked blank, and he even forgot to resent the dribble of Sue's tears inside his collar. " I should have thought that Dave had more sense. I'm eight years younger than he is, but I would have known better than do a stupid thing like that."

" Perhaps Dave knew better, only his heart was kinder than his head," replied Sue with spirit, and Ned stared at her in astonishment. It was not usual for Sue to stand up for Dave. She left that to Nell.

" Well, can't Jim Peters pay ? " he asked.

" He can't if those pearls are stolen. Don't you see he can't ? " wailed Sue in a fresh burst of grief.

" Best set the police on the job ; they'll catch the fellow," said Ned more hopefully than he felt. Then he asked, " Where is Nell, and why hasn't she done the milking ? "

" Nell went over to Scarth Point early this morning to get the Judsons to phone for the doctor, and she has not come back yet. Then Serge Dobbin went out soon after breakfast, and after he had gone we found that Jim's belt was missing, and oh, it has been a most fearful day."

" Here, dry up, Sue, dry up ! " burst out Ned hastily. " Give me your pinafore, because I can't milk with my school clothes on. And after I've milked I'll ride over to Scarth Point to see why Nell has not come back. Make haste ! "

Sue whisked off her pinafore and fastened it on Ned. She had been so afraid of having to milk that the relief of knowing Ned would do it for her made her feel almost light-hearted again.   While he was milking she ran out to the paddock and caught the old horse so that he should not be kept waiting.   She even thought to run indoors and get a big wedge of cake that he might have something to eat on the way.

" While I'm there, I'll just call up the police station and put them on to the job of catching Serge Dobbin," said Ned, when he came back from milking.   " What is the guy like ? "

" Oh, he is a nasty, mean-looking little man, with dark hair and fishy eyes," began Sue ; but Ned pulled her up hastily.

" I can't give that description over the wire.   Small, did you say he was, and dark ? "

" Yes, yes," cried Sue.   " He has a little way of spreading his hands when he talks, and he clips his words off short.   Oh, Ned, how happy we could be if he was caught, because then Jim would have his pearls again, and he could pay what he owes, then Dave would be free."

" It is to be hoped that Dave will learn a lesson and have more sense than to do a thing like that again," grumbled Ned, as he pulled the pinafore over his head to save the trouble of unfastening it.   Then he clambered on to the back of the old horse and rode away in the sunset glow.

He was not long in getting to Scarth Point, but he only found that Nell had left there early in the day to walk to Lupton for the doctor. Mrs. Judson was dreadfully dismayed when she found that Nell had not yet reached home.

" I will ride on to Lupton and fetch the doctor myself," said Ned, frowning heavily, for by this time he was beginning to get the wind up pretty badly on Nell's account.

" No, you will not," said Mrs. Judson with brisk decision. " You will go back home as fast as you can, and you will stay with your aunt and Sue till morning. Poor dears, they must be worried stiff, and they are not to be left alone to-night—do you understand that ? Then when daylight comes you ride from your place straight to Lupton to fetch the doctor, and if Nell has not been heard of, you go for police help."

" I will do it," said Ned, and he said no more ; but turning the horse round he rode back home as fast as he could get the old horse along.

Aunt Angelina Ann came out to meet him, and she cried out in dismay at his news.

" I was sure something must have happened to Nell," she said, her plump face convulsed with grief. " Oh, I was sure that something had happened, or she would never have stayed away so long when we need her so badly. But Mrs. Judson is right : we can't do anything to-night. Come in, sonny, and get your supper, then go to bed and get a good sleep, for you may need all your strength to-morrow."

" I'd rather ride straight off to Lupton now," said Ned, who had gone very white in the face. " I can't go off to bed just as if nothing was the matter, it looks so unfeeling—when, perhaps, poor Nell may be in the most awful trouble."

" She may be, and on the other hand she may not," said Aunt Angelina Ann; " but seeing that you can't help her by sitting up to-night, the best thing for you to do is to get so rested that you can help her better to-morrow."

CHAPTER IX

WHERE IS NELL?

JIM PETERS had lain all day in a kind of stupor; when he roused at all he was mostly more or less off his head from sheer weakness, but he had not suffered from fits of wild delirium since the previous night.

Poor Aunt Angelina Ann was nearly dropping with tiredness, but she managed to keep smiling—she even managed to keep her voice sounding cheerful, which was perhaps a harder task still. It was in the morning after Serge Dobbin had crept out into the sunshine saying he wanted to go for a little walk just to try his legs, that she had found Jim's belt was missing. Jim had flung himself about so wildly in his fits of delirium that the broomstick had wriggled askew, and was sticking out in a way that must hurt the man who had so much to bear. So when Aunt Angelina Ann washed his face and hands, she proceeded to unroll his bandaging to fasten the broomstick in its place again, and it was then that she found the belt was gone.

It was of no use to talk to Jim about it—the poor fellow was not conscious enough to be bothered or disturbed by the story of such a loss; but, hastily covering him up again, the old lady went out to the kitchen, and dropping into a chair by the table, she broke down and sobbed in her misery.

"Is the poor man dead, Auntie?" asked Sue, very white in the face, as she came creeping close to the old lady.

"Good gracious, no!" said Aunt Angelina Ann with explosive force. "I think he is better than he was a couple of hours ago, but the poor dear has been robbed by that rascally little hound Serge Dobbin—robbed under my very nose, so to speak—and I'm so upset about it that I don't feel as if I could ever look him in the face again, poor fellow!"

"Of what has he been robbed?" said Sue blankly, for she had not been told about the belt with pockets which Jim had been wearing.

"I found a belt round Jim's waist," sobbed Aunt Angelina Ann. "I was sure that it had pearls in the pockets, and I left it where I found it, thinking it would be safest there tucked away under all those bandages. Then I found Serge Dobbin trying to get the bandages off when poor Jim was asleep, and I drove Serge out of the room and bolted the door so that he could only get in by coming round through the kitchen. I told Nell about it too, and that is why she would not let you do any outdoor work yesterday, but made you stay in the house with me so that I should not be left alone. But last night, when Jim was so bad, Serge came in of his own accord, and he helped us so well that I said he could stay with me while Nell went to lie down—she looked so worn out, poor child, and she was so scared too, though she would not own to it. Jim got quieter after that, and I dozed a bit. Indeed, once or twice I must have gone off sound asleep, for I nearly fell out of my chair, and Serge came and put a pillow under me, and propped me up so that I would be more comfortable. I thought it was so kind of him, and I had clean forgotten that there was any reason why he should not be allowed to help me, so I dropped asleep again, and that time I must have gone off good and sound, for it was daylight when I woke, to find Jim had a restless turn on him. He was crying and moaning dreadful, and he seemed to be so very ill that I woke Nell to get her off to Scarth Point as quick as I could."

" Don't you worry, Auntie, it will all come right; I'm sure it will." Sue spoke not so much from conviction as from a feeling that Aunt Angelina Ann must not be allowed to despair. The stout woman was just now the prop on which the house leaned : if she gave way, then the whole structure would come crashing about their ears. Oh, she must be kept up somehow. To this end Sue stoutly maintained that the pearls would most certainly be found again, and found very soon, so why worry ?

She succeeded better than she knew. The old aunt left off sobbing, and presently declared that she felt much better. She washed her face and brushed her hair. She tied a clean apron on her ample figure ; she went back to the room where Jim Peters lay, and she put her care behind her, ministering to him with such calm efficiency that his poor overwrought brain felt the comfort of her strength, and rested on it.

It was Sue who bore hard things that day. She was used to work, and she did it bravely and without complaint. Every one in her world worked, so it was no hardship to her that she should have to do likewise ;

but she was not used to worry, and when hour after hour dragged by without a sign of Nell coming back, and with Serge Dobbin still missing—well, her frame of mind might be better imagined than described. But she was always smiling when she came near her aunt—indeed once or twice she contrived to hum the fragment of a gay little song—and if this pose of there being nothing to worry about did not deceive either of them into thinking there was any truth in it, at least it made the trouble easier to bear. And so the long day dragged its length until Ned came home.

When he came back from Scarth Point to report that Nell had gone to Lupton and yet had not brought the doctor, black trouble certainly did drop on Sue again ; but again it had to be forced into the background for the sake of the poor old aunt, who again to-night could not go to bed because of poor Jim Peters.

She and Ned volunteered to stay with him while Aunt Angelina Ann took her supper in leisurely comfort in the kitchen. Sue did not feel so much afraid of Jim when Ned was there. Ned might be younger than herself, but he had such an air of assurance that Sue felt he was quite equal to any occasion, and so was at peace.

Jim had been lying for a long time as if in a stupor, then he roused himself, and in quite a natural tone he asked for Nell.

" She will be here later on, but she has not come back yet. We hope she won't be long," said Sue, with such fervour of yearning in her tone that Jim was at once struck by it, for he was quite conscious now.

" Is anything the matter ? " he asked, lifting his

head a little; and then catching sight of Ned, he jerked out another question : " Who is that boy ? "

" That is Ned, our brother," said Sue, with a wave of her hand meant as introduction, while Ned grinned, but, being shy, did not venture on any other greeting.

Jim's head dropped back on the pillow. " I did not know you had a brother," he said with the air of not caring very much either.

" We have two," explained Sue a little shrilly. Her voice was sharp because she was not sure that it was right for Jim to talk, or to be talked to. " There is David, the eldest—David Nelson Draycot he is, and he is twenty."

" Is David Draycot your brother ? " shouted Jim, with such excitement in his tone that Sue was scared and called for Aunt Angelina Ann, who came hurrying into the room as fast as her bulk would allow.

" Come, come ; you must not let yourself go like this," she said soothingly, letting her big hands drop with a soothing touch on his forehead. She expected to find it very hot, and was at once relieved and comforted to find it cool and moist. " Try and keep quiet for the sake of your leg ; you don't give it a chance, you know, when you are so restless."

" I'm quiet enough, don't you worry, Auntie." One of Jim's hands stole up to catch at the large hand pressed so soothingly on his head. " I only called out because I was so surprised and so glad to find that you are David Draycot's people. I struck it lucky, I did, when I fell into your hands, because now I can rest in peace till my leg is better, while you let David know that I've got the wherewithal to pay what I owe."

Aunt Angelina Ann choked back a groan. Oh, it

was much more awful than she had ever imagined it
would be, to think the poor fellow had to be told that
his pearls were gone—stolen by that mean little wretch,
Serge Dobbin, while she slept at her post.   Oh, it was
truly almost more than she could bear !

Sue reached over and gave her aunt a loving pat
on the arm, and even Ned nodded as if to show his
sympathy ; but Jim was still holding on to the old
lady's hand, and he was saying—oh, what was he
saying ?

"Where is Nell ? Oh, I remember you said she
had gone for the doctor and wasn't back yet. I hope
she won't be long.   I don't like to think of her wandering about at night with all those pearls on her."

"What do you mean ? " shrieked Sue, but the hands
of Aunt Angelina Ann dropped with compelling force
on Jim as she murmured soothingly—

"There, there, lad, keep calm ; just you take things
quiet for a bit."

"Oh, I am quiet enough," said Jim with an easy
laugh ; "but last night when I was alone with Nell I
just slipped my belt off and made her strap it on
under her woolly jacket thing.   I thought that it was
as safe a hiding-place as any I knew, and if old Serge
got peeping and pulling at my clothes to find it when
I was asleep, why, he would just get taken in over it—
that was all.   Ha, ha, ha ! I did him that time.   But
I wish that Nell was home.   I don't like to think that
she is wandering about in the dark.   Why did you
not send her for the doctor sooner ? "

"Do you mean that our Nell has your pearls ? " cried
Aunt Angelina Ann, in such amazement, relief, and joy
that the words seemed to literally fall out of her mouth.

" That is just what I do mean," he said, with such peace and rest in his tone that they were all convinced he knew what he was talking about. " I feel so drowsy that I think I will have a nap, but mind that you rouse me when Nell comes."

" We will do that," promised the old lady, and then he was asleep, while the three of them stole out of the kitchen, where they hugged each other all round just to show how glad they were that the pearls had not been stolen by Serge Dobbin.

" I wish we knew why Nell had not come home," sighed Sue.

" So do I," replied her aunt, echoing the sigh. " But we have got to wait for morning, and so it is up to us to wait as patiently and as cheerfully as we can. Get the supper dishes cleared away as quickly as you can, and then be off to bed, both of you. Jim is so much better to-night that I shall not need any help. I wonder where that man Serge has gone. I suppose he'll not be coming back to-night ? "

" Jiminy, do you expect he is out looking for our Nell and the pearls ? " cried Ned, jumping round the kitchen in a perfect panic.

" Why should he be ? " said Aunt Angelina Ann with a serene air, and then she went back to the bed-room where Jim lay. Of course Serge would not be wandering round looking for Nell, because he would not know that she had the pearls. If he had looked to find them last night and had discovered that they were gone, he would only think that they had been hidden somewhere about the house.

In that case the wonder was that he had not stayed in the house on the chance of finding the place where they had been hidden. Oh, it was a worry. If only it was morning and time for Ned to start for the town !

All through the long hours of the night the fears of Aunt Angelina Ann were mounting and mounting ; she fought them as hard as she could, but she fought a losing battle. Tired though she was she could not rest—she never even dozed, though Jim slumbered peacefully and only stirred when she roused him to take nourishment.

With the first light of dawning she had Ned out of bed, and bidding him do the milking first, because Sue was so afraid of the cows, she told him that he must go to Lupton at once, and that he must go to the police if the doctor could give him no news of Nell.

Ned rode to Lupton at breakneck pace, but when he halted his panting horse at the doctor's house it was to be told that Nell Draycot had not been there on the previous day, and nothing was known of her whereabouts.

Staying only long enough to ask that the doctor would go as early as he could to the Draycot homestead, and also to Ben Judson at Scarth Point, Ned turned the head of the old horse in the direction of the police station, and there he told his story, asking for help in finding Nell.

CHAPTER X

NELL'S first impulse on recognizing Serge Dobbin was
to turn and flee. Second thoughts told her that flight
at that moment might be more dangerous than staying
where she was. It was dark, and the rank growths of
that neglected patch of garden ground reached right
up to her waist. All she had to do to be effectually
hidden was to sink to her knees in crowding plants and
await developments.

From what she could overhear she judged it was the
driver of the motor-car who was hurt, and very badly
hurt too, while Serge Dobbin and another man who
had been riding in the motor-car had only been slightly
knocked about. Serge had a wound on his leg, and
the other man was very much cut about the face and
head.

" The poor chap can't be left lying here all night,"
said yet another man, whom Nell had not seen before,
but who now straightened himself up from the ground.
" I know what you had better do. There is Neal
Caister's bit of a house just over in that garden-patch ;
we'll carry him there, and you that have got a hurt
leg can stay with him, while you that are only cut
about the face and head can go back a couple of miles

to Swinton's place : they have the telephone, and you will be able to get on to a doctor."

"I can't be left alone with him—why, the fellow might die on my hands," protested the petulant voice of Serge. "Why can't you go back to Swinton's place yourself ? It was your fault that the smash-up came."

"It was not my fault," said the man sternly. "I was on the right side of the road, and I was showing a rear light, but if people will drive like mad when the road goes round a curve, they must expect disaster. I can't go back to Swinton's place ; I can't leave four mettlesome horses standing in the road untended, and I can't turn my load round either. I shan't pass a farm with a phone wire for three hours, and by that time you can have a doctor out here. It is only about twelve or fourteen miles to New Plymouth from here."

"Lend us a hand to carry him to the house, will you then, for my leg threatens to let me down every time I move," grumbled Serge, who groaned as if he was in very bad pain indeed.

"All right, I'll do that," said the man, whose voice was kind though stern. "Just let me go and tie my two front horses to the fence, or they will likely enough start forward on their own, and I shall have to chase them."

Nell could hear the run of his feet on the road ; she heard him talking to his horses, and suddenly she felt that she could trust him. A man who took the trouble to be kind, even friendly, to his animals must certainly be trusted.

It had flashed into her mind that she could get a ride on that timber lorry to the town. He was going to be three hours on the road ; he had said so. Well, where could she be better off during the hours of darkness than perched on that load of tree-trunks, crawling slowly through the night ?

But she could not come forward to ask for a ride while Serge was within earshot. Perhaps she could clamber up and hide herself somewhere on the load while the hurt man was being carried into the house.

They had lifted the hurt man ; he was groaning fearfully ; they were coming towards the spot where she cowered among the tall weeds. For a minute it seemed to her as if they were going to walk straight over her. But no, they passed a little to one side, and immediately they were past she began to squirm through the tangled plants in the direction of the timber lorry.

She reached it. She saw to her great relief that although the bottom of the load was heavy tree-trunks, the top consisted of a mixed medley of hay trusses, great fagots of sweet-smelling spruce and cedar, all green and springy, with crates of cabbages and other sorts of garden stuff.

As agile as a monkey, Nell swung herself up on the back of the load and crouched down between the trusses of hay and the spruce fagots. In daylight she would, of course, have been clearly visible, but now she might hope to pass unnoticed, at least for a little while, and with a wildly beating heart she waited for the driver of the lorry to come out. Suppose for some reason he was to bring Serge Dobbin out with him ! Nell felt that in such a case she would go simply wild with terror. She even regretted the impulse that had made her climb on to the load. She made a movement to climb down again, but just then she heard voices and saw a lantern coming towards her.   It was too late now for repenting ; she had just to lie still and wait.

It was not Serge who was with the driver, but the other man who had a cut face and who was going to the place where he could phone for the doctor.   A minute or two they stood talking, and then the driver of the lorry came to hang the lantern again on the back of his load, for it was his rear light.

Nell hardly dared to breathe while they were standing so close to her.   She wondered if any part of her was visible to them from the light of the lantern that swung from a great piece of timber at the back of the load.   She could not see them, for she had to keep her head well down between two fagots of cedar brush, but she could hear every word they said, and it seemed just dreadful to be eavesdropping.

" You'll find Swinton's all right if you keep to the road," said the driver of the lorry.

" Think the fellow in yonder will live till I get back ? " asked the man with the cut face.

" He may do.   He is desperately bashed up, but it may be mostly surface hurts ; he groans so much that he has plainly a good bit of strength left in him.   The other fellow is a bit of a coward, I should say ; he seems scared stiff at being left."

" He doesn't seem to have an idea about doing things either.   I told him to get a fire going and some water hot ready for the doctor, but whether he'll do it or not I can't say.   I will step lively to Swinton's, and then I'll get back here to see what I can do."

" That is right ; and you know my name and address to give the police, and you can swear that I was on the right side of the road and showing a rear light ? "

" I can that. Oh, you will be all right," said the man with the cut face.

" I ought to be," growled the driver of the lorry. " I give up my night's rest twice a week to do this journey at night, as the day traffic is so heavy on these roads, and it is downright vexing when a crazy chap like that poor fellow we've carried in yonder must needs go and smash himself up against my load like this. Well, so long ; I hope you will be able to get the doctor out in good time."

The two men parted. Nell could hear the quick steps of the man heading for Swinton's place, and she could hear the driver talking to his horses as he unfastened them from the fence. Then he climbed to the driving-seat, and, unhitching the reins from the hook at his side, he started his horses, and with much creaking and groaning of the timber the heavy lorry went slowly forward.

If Nell had stretched out her hand she could have touched the man's head. She nearly gurgled into laughter at the thought of what his astonishment would be. But she had no desire to spring a surprise on him ; she was best pleased to remain hidden for a time.

She was not very comfortable ; her feet were rather higher than her head, a spruce fagot tickled one ear, a cedar fagot scratched the other, while her nose was irritated by the wisps of hay sticking out from the bands round the hay trusses. Yet it might have been worse—oh, so very much worse. She might not have waked in time to get out of the house before the men with their burden came in, and then she would have been face to face with Serge, and she was wearing Jim Peters's belt with the pearls under her frock.

She drew a long breath at the thought of her de-
liverances from the man who was trying so hard to
rob Jim, and then she thought of David, and how
relieved he would be to know that Jim had made
good.

" Get up, Bowler ; gee-up, Turpin ! "

Nell gave such a jump at the sound of the voice so
close to her that she nearly rolled from her perch.
Nearly asleep she must have been, and so the voice
had startled her. She must try to keep awake somehow, or she might come upon very serious disaster
indeed.

The driver talked to his horses a great deal, perhaps
he too was feeling sleepy. Presently he checked them,
and getting down, walked by the side of the front pair,
talking to them as if they had been humans.

This was Nell's opportunity to make her position
more secure, and also more comfortable. She managed
to slide herself under one of the ropes so that she could
not fall off the load ; she also wriggled round so that
she was now with her head higher than her feet. She
was partly under the fagots now, and lying at ease on
the hay, which smelled delightfully fresh and fragrant.
Oh, she was really very comfortable, and——

. . . .

" Hallo ! hallo ! what next, I wonder ? Where did
you come from, and how did you get up here ? "

Nell opened her eyes and tried to think where she
was. She even wondered how the man, peering up at
her, could stretch his neck and goggle his eyes in such
a funny fashion. Then she suddenly remembered all
about everything, especially that she was carrying
Jim's pearls, and running away from Serge Dobbin.

She must have run a good many miles away from him by now, for already it was getting light ; another day had come, and perhaps she was already in New Plymouth, for there were houses now on each side of the road, while a great building like a factory towered skyward in the near distance.

" Where on earth did you come from ? " demanded the driver in an explosive tone. As he spoke he gave a tug at the reins, and his tired horses stopped dead. Trust them for stopping at the very least excuse just now. Then the driver went on in a tone of deep astonishment, " Why, it is a girl ! "

" Of course it is a girl," said Nell calmly, as she struggled to a sitting posture ; and then finding that she was sitting with her back to the man who was questioning her, she rolled on to her knees and so faced him. " I have had a very nice ride, thank you, and I am much obliged to you. I really think I must have been asleep. Is this New Plymouth ? "

" Of course it is New Plymouth. But where do you come from, and how did you get up here ? That is what I want to know, and I'm going to know too."

" Oh, oh, there is a policeman ; call him quick, quick ! " cried Nell, who had spotted a tired constable just coming off duty.

" That is just what I am going to do, Miss, don't you worry," said the man grimly, and then he let out a hail that would have started his horses running away if they had not been so tired.

The constable, a big, heavy man, approached the side of the timber lorry. " What is wrong ? " he asked the driver ; but before that worthy man could open his lips to reply, Nell had reached down from the load, she had seized the big policeman by the shoulder, and she was clutching at the astonished official as if she would never let him go.

" Please, please take me to the police station," she cried. " Catch hold of me tight, and don't let me go until we reach there. I have something of great importance to tell you ; but I must be taken care of. Will you please take the address of this kind man, and then my father will send the money to pay for my ride ? "

" Well, but I want to know how she got there," said the driver, whose eyes were still goggling as he looked from Nell to the policeman.

The big man reached up his arms, and Nell slithered into them. He set her on her feet, but she cried out imploringly, " Don't let me go ; hang on to me until we reach the police station."

It was not often that people came asking to be taken into custody ; still, when they did, they ought to be humoured. So the big constable thought, and his large hand closed in a possessive grip on Nell's shoulder, to her very great delight. In her relief and thankfulness she could have almost hugged him.

" How did she get on my lorry, that is what I want to know ? I hadn't an earthly idea she was there," said the driver, addressing himself now to the constable, for he despaired of getting any information out of Nell.

But she turned to him and answered quietly, " I climbed up on your load while you and the others were carrying the man who had been hurt into Neal Caister's little house. I am sorry that I could not ask your permission ; but my father will pay you for my ride."

" I don't want any money for giving you a lift," said the man in a bewildered tone ; " I only wanted to know how you managed to settle yourself up there without me knowing."

Nell turned to the policeman. " Please take me to the police station as quickly as you can ; my business is urgent," she said.

And with a nod to the driver of the timber lorry, the big policeman marched her away.

.   .   .   .

Mr. and Mrs. Draycot had just received a wire from Lupton ; it came from Ned, and it was very brief :

" Can you come home ?   Nell is lost—police searching.   Ned."

" Whatever shall we do ? " cried Mrs. Draycot.

" We must go, and at once," replied her husband. " I do not think it will hurt David to travel to-day, and if it does we can't help it.   Whatever could Nell have been doing to get lost ?   What a world it is : troubles never seem to come singly—at least ours have not."

" Perhaps this is not a real trouble, though it looks like one," said Mrs. Draycot, who, although she was rather frail and ailing, could yet rise to the occasion in a really wonderful manner.

Mr. Draycot went out from the house where they were staying.   He was on his way to the stables where his horses were kept, to bring up his wagon, but at that moment a policeman appeared and asked him to step along to the police station.

" What is the matter now ? " asked the harassed man.   " The Southern Bank have given my son three weeks to find the money, so it can't be that."

" I should not say that this was trouble," replied
the policeman, who was a young man with a merry
eye. " But the inspector said he wanted to see you
most particular, and at once."

Perhaps Mr. Draycot had never in his life had a
greater surprise than when he went into the police
station to see Nell sitting in what was known as the
common room. She was eating her breakfast, and there
was a big mug of coffee standing by her plate. She
was ragged and dirty beyond belief, but she was Nell,
and when he came into the room she flung herself
into his arms, hugging him in joyous abandon.

" Nell, Nell, what have you been doing ? " he asked,
and there was a petulant ring in his tone, for surely
they had trouble enough with David just now, and
they should have been spared any further worry.
" We have just had a wire from Ned calling us home
because you are lost, and the police searching for you.
We are just going to start for home, and we are taking
David with us, though I fear the poor fellow is not
fit to travel."

" He will be fit enough when he sees me, and hears
what I have to tell him," said Nell blithely. " You
can't start for home, Daddy, until bank opens. I
shall be in custody until then. The inspector has
promised that two policemen shall take me in a taxi
to the Southern Bank ; for Jim Peters has come back,
and I have got his pearls here—twenty thousand
pounds' worth or thereabouts—so David will not have
to find the money after all."

" Thank God for that ! " exclaimed Mr. Draycot in
a deeply moved tone. " It would have meant taking
up a mortgage on the homestead, and it is the worry

of it that has made David so ill. He had got a hundred pounds saved, but he had no more, and I could not have managed to raise the other hundred except by mortgage. But, Nell, you can't go to the bank looking like that ! "

" I can, and I must," said Nell, but she looked a little rueful ; it was just horrid to be so untidy. " The inspector said I was to go just as I am."

The journey home did not hurt David in the least—in fact, he grew better with every hour that passed. The Southern Bank had given Nell a receipt which she was to give to Jim Peters, and she wore it in a bag next to her heart. What a journey it was ! She had never been so happy in her life.

She was not even afraid of Serge Dobbin, for when the inspector had heard her story, he told her that he had already sent some men out to arrest him, as information had come from Australia that he was wanted for some law-breaking of a serious character on the mainland, and hence New Zealand would be quit of him for a very long time indeed.

And that was how Nell scored.

THE END

PRINTED IN GREAT BRITAIN AT
THE PRESS OF THE PUBLISHERS